Miss Aker Is a Maker!

Dan Gutman

Pictures by
Jim Paillot

An Impr

To the kids at Calvin Coolidge
Elementary School in Wyckoff,
New Jersey

Warning: This book contains
scenes of graphic violins. If you
don't like graphic violins,
READ SOMETHING ELSE!

My Weirder-est School #8: Miss Aker Is a Maker!
Text copyright © 2021 by Dan Gutman
Illustrations copyright © 2021 by Jim Paillot
For information address HarperCollins Children's Books, a division of
HarperCollins Publishers, 195 Broadway, New York, NY 10007.
www.harpercollinschildrens.com

ISBN 978-0-06-291044-8 (pbk bdg.) — ISBN 978-0-06-291077-6 (library bdg.)

Typography by Martha Maynard
21 22 23 24 25   PC/LSCH   10 9 8 7 6 5 4 3 2 1
❖
First Edition

Contents

1. MM   1

2. The Fab Lab   11

3. Making Droney   22

4. Droney Is Cool   30

5. We're Gonna Be Famous!   38

6. We Created a Monster!   53

7. An Important Message . . .   65

8. This Means War!   68

9. D-Day   81

10. The Big Surprise Ending   95

MM

My name is A.J., and I know what you're thinking. You're thinking about dogs in elevators. Because that's what I'm thinking about.

Do dogs know that elevators go up and down? Why would they? If I was a dog and I got into an elevator, how would I know it went up and down? I would just think it was a cool magic room. You walk into it, some human pushes a button, and the next thing you know, the door opens up and you walk out into this completely different place. Like magic! Why would I know any better? I'm a dog! What do I know about elevators?

It must be great to be a dog and go into magical rooms all the time at the push of a button.

Anyway, the other day at school, we were about to start a math lesson when we got called down to the all-porpoise room.*

---

*I don't know why they call it the all-porpoise room. There aren't any dolphins in there.

Our teacher, Mr. Cooper, said there was going to be a surprise assembly.

Surprises are always fun, except for the ones that aren't so much fun. Like if an elephant fell on your head. That would be surprising, but not much fun.

"Ooooh, I love surprises!" said Andrea Young, this annoying girl with curly brown hair.

"Me too!" said her crybaby friend, Emily, who loves everything Andrea loves.

When we got to the all-porpoise room, I noticed something weird. Our principal, Mr. Klutz, was wearing a T-shirt with the letters *MM* on it.

"What do you think MM stands for?" I asked.

"March Madness?" replied Michael, who never ties his shoes.

"Marilyn Monroe?" said Ryan, who will eat anything, even stuff that isn't food.

"Mickey Mouse?" said Neil, who we call the nude kid even though he wears clothes.

"My Mom?" said Alexia, this girl who rides a skateboard all the time.

Everybody was buzzing, which was weird because we're not bees.

Mr. Klutz made a peace sign with his fingers, which means "Shut up!"

We all got quiet.

"Good morning, students," he said. "Do you know why it says MM on my shirt?"

"You're giving out M&M's?" I asked.

"I love M&M's," Ryan whispered to me.

"Me too," I whispered back.

M&M's are great. Not as great as Kit Kats, but they're still chocolate, so you know they're good. Anything with chocolate in it is good. That's the first rule of being a kid.

"You could cover a piece of dirt with chocolate and I would eat it," said Ryan. Of course, Ryan will eat *anything*.

"*No*," said Mr. Klutz. "We're not giving out M&M's."

"Boo!" Everybody started booing.

Mr. Klutz made the shut-up peace sign again, and we got quiet.

"Let me explain," he said. "Kids today spend too much time staring at screens. TV screens. Smartphone screens. Screens on tablets. *Blah blah blah* getting soft *blah blah blah* lazy *blah blah blah* nobody *does* anything anymore. You just stare at screens. That's not good for you *blah blah blah*."

He went on and on.

"So you're going to give us M&M's if we stop staring at screens?" I asked.

"No," said Mr. Klutz. "MM stands for the Maker Movement."

Maker Movement? I'd never heard of the Maker Movement.

"What's that?" somebody shouted.

"I'm glad you asked," said Mr. Klutz. "Miss Aker, will you come out here, please?"

Some lady came out on the stage. We gave her a round of applause even though she hadn't done anything yet. What's up with that? All she did was walk out on the stage. Anybody can walk out on a stage.

Mr. Klutz told us Miss Aker is on the PTA, which stands for Parents who Talk A lot. He said Miss Aker used to be in the army, and now she's an engineer.

"She drives trains?" I asked.

"Not *that* kind of engineer, dumbhead!" said Andrea.

I was going to say something mean to Andrea, but I didn't get the chance, because Miss Aker started talking.

"The Maker Movement is all about making things," said Miss Aker. "*Blah blah blah* innovation and creativity *blah blah blah* let your imagination run wild *blah blah blah* think outside the box and solve real-world problems *blah blah blah*. We're going to learn by *doing* things!"

What?! Doing things? Doing things is hard work! If you ask me, it's a lot easier to *not* do things.

"And *that's* why it says MM on my shirt today," said Mr. Klutz.

"I love making things!" said Andrea. "I'm making a birdhouse at home."

Ugh. Why can't a truck full of birdhouses fall on Andrea's head?

"Me too!" said Emily, who does everyhing Andrea does. What is their problem?

The guys and I were moaning and aning. I don't want to make stuff. Makstuff sounds boring.

aking things is *fun*!" said Miss Aker.

"We're going to make all *kinds* of interesting things. We're going to have a Maker Space in the school. And we're going to have a Maker Fair to show off the things you make. Doesn't the Maker Movement sound like fun?"

"Yes!" shouted all the girls.

"No!" shouted all the boys.

The Maker Movement? *Bowel* movement is more like it.

I'd rather have M&M's.

The Fab Lab

After the assembly, we walked a million hundred miles back to Mr. Cooper's class. He wears a cape and thinks he's a super-hero. Nobody knows why.

"Turn to page twenty-three in your math books," said Mr. Cooper.

Ugh. I hate math. I got out my math

book. But you'll never believe who walked into the door at that moment.

Nobody! You could break your nose by walking into a door. But you'll never believe who walked into the door*way*.

It was Miss Aker!

"Hey kids!" she shouted. "It's Maker Movement time! Follow me!"

Mr. Cooper slammed his math book shut. We all followed Miss Aker and walked a million hundred miles.

"Where are we going?" asked Alexia.

"To a secret room," said Miss Aker.

Oooh, secret rooms are cool, because they have secrets in them.*

Miss Aker led us to a locked door. I had never been in this room before. I heard a rumor that it was a dungeon where bad kids get tortured. Miss Aker used a key to unlock the door. It opened with a creak.

"I'm scared," said Emily, who's scared of everything.

---

*That is, except for secrets like an elephant is about to secretly fall on your head. That wouldn't be cool.

Miss Aker flipped on the light.

"Welcome to our Maker Space!" she said excitedly. "I call it the Fab Lab, because it's fabulous."

You won't believe what was in the Fab Lab. The shelves were filled with boxes of plastic cups, Ping-Pong balls, PVC pipe, Popsicle sticks, string, clothespins, paper clips, straws, balloons, bottle caps, duct tape, paper bags, plastic bottles, Q-tips, rubber bands, toothpicks, masking tape, glue, tacks, and all kinds of other stuff. What a bunch of junk!

"Is it garbage day?" I asked.

"No!" said Miss Aker. "We can use these things to make other things."

That's when our art teacher, Ms. Hannah, came into the room. She was carrying a box of those tubes that are inside rolls of toilet paper.

"I never throw *anything* away," said Ms. Hannah.

People who save toilet paper tubes are weird. Ms. Hannah is bananas.

"Put them over there," said Miss Aker. "Thank you for making a donation to the Fab Lab."

"You're welcome," said Ms. Hannah. "Everything can be made into something else."

"That's right!" said Miss Aker. "Making things is a basic human drive. Back in the

Stone Age, primitive people made tools so they could hunt and build shelters. And people have been making things ever since *blah blah blah blah blah blah...*"

Miss Aker sure talks a lot. No wonder she's on the PTA.

"Are we going to make something *today*?" asked Ryan.

"Of course!" said Miss Aker. "We can make just about *anything*—a soda-bottle airplane, friendship bracelets, a solar blimp, a rubber-band helicopter . . ."

"Can we make a skateboard?" Alexia asked.

"Sure!" said Miss Aker.

"I don't want to make a skateboard," said Andrea.

"Me neither," said Emily, who only wants to make stuff Andrea wants to make.

"Can we make a car?" asked Michael.

"Sure!" said Miss Aker.

"Cars are boring," said Andrea. "Can we make cupcakes?"

"Sure!" said Miss Aker. "I have all the

ingredients on the shelf over there. And an oven too."

"Cupcakes are boring," said Neil.

"We need to make something *everybody* will like," said Miss Aker. "I have an idea! Why don't we make cupcake cars?"

Cupcake cars?

"A cupcake car is a car made out of a cupcake!" said Miss Aker.

So it has the perfect name.

"YAY!" everybody yelled, which is also "YAY" backward. "Let's make cupcake cars!"

Miss Aker showed us how to make cupcakes. First we mixed up the batter. Then we put it into metal molds in the shape of a car. Then we put them in the oven and baked them. Then we took them out of the oven and put Oreo wheels on them with toothpicks.

It was fun making cupcake cars. And the best part was, while we were baking them, Miss Aker let *me* lick the bowl! YAY! It was the best moment of my life. Licking a bowl is great.

Well, not *all* bowls. I mean, you wouldn't want to lick a toilet bowl. That would be gross. And you wouldn't want to lick a bowling alley. That would be weird.

"I'm going to bring my cupcake car home to show to my parents," said Andrea after we put on the Oreo wheels.

"Me too," said Emily.

"You can do whatever you want with your cupcake car," said Miss Aker.

"I'm going to eat mine!" I said.

"Me too!" said Michael.

Ryan, Michael, Neil, Alexia, and I ate our cupcake cars. They were still warm. Yum!

I always wanted to eat a car.

Hey, maybe the Maker Movement won't be so bad after all.

Making Droney

The next morning, Mr. Cooper came running into class, tripped over somebody's backpack, and almost crashed into the garbage can. Mr. Cooper is no superhero. In fact, he's the opposite of a superhero. He got up and brushed himself off.

"Okay, let's get started," said Mr. Cooper. "We have a lot of ground to make up. Turn to page twenty-three in your math books."

Ugh. I got out my math book. But you'll never believe who poked her head into the door at that moment.

Nobody! Why would you poke your head into a door? Doors are made out of wood. I thought we went over that in Chapter Two. But you'll never believe who poked her head into the door*way*.

It was Miss Aker!

"Hey kids!" she shouted. "It's Maker Movement time! Follow me!"

Mr. Cooper slammed his math book

shut, closed his eyes, and rubbed his fore-head. Grown-ups are always rubbing their foreheads. If you ask me, they need to use moisturizer.

"What are we going to make today, Miss Aker?" asked Andrea as we walked to the Fab Lab.

"Can we make more cupcake cars?" Ryan asked. "They were yummy."

"We made cupcake cars yesterday," said Miss Aker. "Let's make something differ-ent today."

The door to the Fab Lab was already open. And you'll never believe who was in there.

It was Mrs. Yonkers, our computer teacher!

"I have a donation for the Fab Lab," said Mrs. Yonkers as she plugged some weird-looking machine into an outlet.

"Thank you!" said Miss Aker. "The teachers have been *so* generous."

"What is it?" we all asked.

"It's a 3D printer," explained Mrs. Yonkers. "Back in the olden days, you could only use a computer to print on *paper.* Now we can print *objects.*"

"Like what kind of objects?" asked Neil.

"Just about *anything,*"

replied Mrs. Yonkers. "You could make replacement parts for a broken toy. Or a statue. Or a doll. I thought you kids might be able to come up with some fun ideas."

3D printing sounded cool.

"Could you use a 3D printer to print out *another* 3D printer?" I asked. "It would be cool to print a printer on your printer."

"I don't see why not," said Mrs. Yonkers.

"Could we print a robot?" I suggested. Robots are cool.

"That's a marvelous idea!" said Miss Aker.

And you'll never believe who walked into the door at that moment.

Nobody! People don't walk into doors.* But you'll never believe who walked into the door*way*.

It was Mr. Docker, our science teacher.

"Did somebody say *robot*?" asked Mr. Docker.

"I did," I said.

"I *love* robots!" said Mr. Docker and Mrs. Yonkers at the same time.

We all agreed that making a robot on the 3D printer would be cool.

"I have an idea," said Ryan. "Let's make a *flying* robot!"

"I have an idea," said Neil. "Let's make a flying robot that can *talk*!"

---

*You should really pay more attention when you read.

"I have an idea," said Andrea. "Let's make a flying, talking robot that's really *smart*!"

"I have an idea," said Alexia. "Let's make a flying, talking robot that's really smart and can shoot marshmallows!"

We had lots of ideas. Mr. Docker and Mrs. Yonkers used the computer to help us design a smart robot that could fly, talk, and shoot marshmallows. We all worked on it as a team. It took a long time. But I didn't mind, because we were getting out of math.

When we were finished designing our robot, we printed it on the 3D printer.

"We should give our robot a name,"

Andrea said as the robot was printing.

We all threw out names: Mr. Flying Robot. Robo-Marsh. Maker-Man. Flo-Bot.

"Y'know," said Ryan, "a flying robot is sort of like a drone."

"We should name it Droney," said Neil.

Droney! Everybody agreed that would be a great name. Neil should get the Nobel Prize. That's a prize they give out to people who don't have bells.

Droney Is Cool

We worked so hard making Droney that we lost track of the time. We even skipped lunch. It was almost three o'clock. That's when Mr. Klutz came into the Fab Lab.

"I just wanted to see how you kids were making out," he said.

Ewww, gross!

"We're not making out!" we all shouted.

"No," said Mr. Klutz. "You're part of the Maker Movement, so I wanted to see how you were *making* out. Get it? Maker Movement? *Making* out?"

We all laughed, even though it wasn't funny. Always laugh at the principal's jokes, even if they're not funny. That's the first rule of being a kid.

Mr. Klutz looked at Droney.

"What's this?" he asked.

"It's a wireless, radio-controlled, speech-synthesized flying robot," explained Miss Aker. "We made it."

"And we named it Droney," said Ryan. "It shoots marshmallows."

"Cool!" said Mr. Klutz. "I'm so proud of you kids. You're really getting into the spirit of the Maker Movement."

"We were about to test Droney," said Miss Aker. "Would you like to watch, Mr. Klutz?"

"You bet!" he said.

Mr. Docker tinkered with Droney's motor. Mrs. Yonkers adjusted Droney's propellers. Miss Aker flipped Droney's ON switch. And slowly, Droney rose up off the table and hovered in the air.

"WOW," said Mr. Klutz, which is "MOM" upside down. "How do you control it? Is there a remote?"

"No, we control it with voice commands,"

said Miss Aker. "Speak, Droney!"

"HELLO," Droney said in a computery voice. "MY NAME IS DRONEY."

"It talks?" said Mr. Klutz.

"It's smart too!" said Miss Aker. "Watch this. Droney, who invented the Band-Aid?"

"THE BAND-AID WAS INVENTED IN 1920 BY EARLE DICKSON IN NEW JERSEY," said Droney.

"We downloaded the entire internet into Droney's memory," said Mrs. Yonkers. "So it knows *everything*."

"I AM SMARTER THAN ANY HUMAN BEING," said Droney.

"Gee, Droney is kind of full of itself," I said.

"Yeah, Droney shouldn't brag," said Andrea. "Bragging isn't nice."

"I HEARD THAT," said Droney.

"I guess we should have programmed Droney to be more modest," Miss Aker whispered.

"MR. KLUTZ," said Droney, "WOULD YOU LIKE TO ARM WRESTLE?"

Mr. Klutz laughed. He's a big, strong man, and it seemed kind of silly for him to arm wrestle a robot half his size.

"Oh, I don't want to break you," said Mr. Klutz.

"DON'T WORRY," said Droney. "IF I GET HURT, THE KIDS CAN PRINT OUT A NEW ARM ON THE 3D PRINTER."

Good point. Droney hovered next to

the table. Mr. Klutz got into position. Miss Aker put Mr. Klutz's hand against Droney's claw hand.

"This will be a piece of cake," Mr. Klutz whispered to us.*

"Okay," said Miss Aker. "Ready? Set? GO!"

Mr. Klutz and Droney pushed their arms against each other. They were pushing really hard.

"Droney is *strong*!" Mr. Klutz groaned as his hand was pushed back. It hit the table, and then Mr. Klutz fell on the floor.

"Droney wins!" we all shouted.

---

*What does cake have to do with anything? Why is everybody always talking about cake?

"Owwwww!" groaned Mr. Klutz. "I think I sprained my arm."

"I AM STRONGER THAN ANY HUMAN BEING," announced Droney.

Wow, Droney is like a superhero with superpowers! We all gathered around Mr. Klutz and helped him off the floor.

"I AM *BETTER* THAN EVERY HUMAN BEING," announced Droney.

"Well, I don't know about *that*!" said Mr. Klutz as he rubbed his shoulder.

We all laughed nervously. And then suddenly . . .

Briiiiiinnnnnnggggg!

It was the dismissal bell. Time to go home.

We're Gonna Be Famous!

When we got to Mr. Cooper's class the next morning, he was already there, sitting with his feet up on his desk and playing a violin. That was weird. I didn't even know Mr. Cooper played violin. He was playing a sad song.

"Uh . . . should we pledge the allegiance?" Ryan asked.

"If you want," Mr. Cooper replied without looking up.

"Are we going to do Word of the Day?" asked Michael.

"I don't care," mumbled Mr. Cooper.

"Should we turn to page twenty-three in our math books?" asked Alexia.

"Whatever," he replied.

"Are you okay, Mr. Cooper?" asked Andrea.

"Just go to the Fab Lab," he muttered. "That's where you're going to end up anyway."

That was weird. We pringled up.

"What's wrong with Mr. Cooper?" asked Emily as we walked to the Fab Lab.

"I think he's sad because we're spending

so much time with Miss Aker," said Andrea. Andrea's mom is a psychologist, so she thinks she knows everything.

Finally, we got to the Fab Lab.

"Hey kids!" Miss Aker shouted. "It's Maker Movement time!"

"What are we going to make today?" asked Alexia.

"Today we're going to—"

But Miss Aker didn't have the chance to finish her sentence. Because that's when the weirdest thing in the history of the world happened. A lady walked into the room.

Well, that's not the weird part. Ladies walk into rooms all the time. The weird part was what happened after that.

The lady looked familiar. She was wearing an old-timey man's hat and a trench coat. There was a camera around her neck and a notepad in her hand. I knew I had seen her before.

"It's Mrs. Lilly!" Emily shouted.

Emily was right! Mrs. Lilly is a reporter for our local paper, *The News Tribune Bulletin Inquirer.*

"Hiya kids," said Mrs. Lilly. "I got a hot tip that your school is part of the Maker Movement, and you made a robot. Is it true?"

"Yes!" we shouted.

"Are you going to put us in the newspaper?" asked Andrea.

"Why not?" said Mrs. Lilly. "I'm always

on the lookout for a good human-interest story."

I'm sure Andrea was imagining her picture in the paper and Mrs. Lilly's article up on the refrigerator in Andrea's kitchen. Her mom was sure to buy copies to send to all their relatives.

I looked out the window and saw a big limo pull up to the front of the school. A lady got out, followed by a bunch of guys with camera equipment.

I recognized the lady. She was the famous TV producer Ms. Beard. One time, she came to our school and filmed a reality show called *The Real Teachers of Ella Mentry School.* Ms. Beard came rushing into our class with her camera crew.

"Are you the kids who made a robot on a 3D printer?" she asked.

"Yes," said Neil. "Are you going to put us on TV?"

"Sure!" said Ms. Beard. "I'm always on the lookout for a good human-interest story."

Everybody freaked out.

"We're gonna be on TV!" shouted Alexia.

"We're gonna be famous!" shouted Neil.

"How do I look?" asked Andrea. "I have to fix my hair."

"Why?" I asked. "Is your hair broken?"

Andrea rolled her eyes. The crew was running around, setting up lights, cameras, and microphones all over the Fab Lab. Andrea kept moving so she would be in front of the camera at all times.

"This is going to be *fabulous*," said Ms. Beard. "Our ratings are going to go through the roof!"

"What do you want us to do?" asked Andrea.

"Just act normal, Chickie Baby!" said Ms. Beard. "This is reality TV. We don't use scripts. Nobody has lines. We just see what happens and film it."

I remembered that Ms. Beard calls everybody "Chickie Baby." Nobody knows why.

That's when Mr. Klutz came into the Fab Lab. His arm was in a sling because of the arm-wrestling contest with Droney.

"What's all the commotion about?" Mr. Klutz asked.

"Mrs. Lilly and Ms. Beard are going to put us in the newspaper and on TV!" said Andrea. She and Emily were jumping up and down with excitement.

"TV?" asked Mr. Klutz.

He started adjusting his tie and smoothing out his shirt. I'm sure he would have combed his hair, too, if he *had* any hair.

"Welcome back to Ella Mentry School, ladies," he said, smiling sweetly. "I'm the principal. If there's anything I can do to—"

"Fabulous, Chickie Baby!" said Ms. Beard. "Let's do lunch sometime."

Mrs. Lilly was walking around the Fab Lab, looking at things and jotting down notes in her pad.

"What happened to your arm?" she asked Mr. Klutz.

"I was arm wrestling with Droney and

things got . . . out of hand," he said.

"So you got into a fight with the drone?" Mrs. Lilly was writing furiously in her notebook.

"Not exactly," said Mr. Klutz. "What happened was—"

"I can see the headline now," interrupted Mrs. Lilly. "PRINCIPAL BREAKS ARM IN SAVAGE DRONE ATTACK!"

"My arm isn't broken," said Mr. Klutz. "It's just a little sore."

"How's this for a catchy headline?" asked Mrs. Lilly. "PRINCIPAL MAY DIE!"

"But . . . but . . . but . . ." said Mr. Klutz.

We all started giggling because Mr. Klutz said "but," which sounds just like "butt" even though it only has one *T*.*

Ms. Beard was ready to start filming.

"Okay," she shouted. "Quiet on the set! Lights! Camera! Everybody act normal. ACTION!" Then she jumped in front of the camera.

"This is Ms. Beard, reporting to you from Ella Mentry School," she said. "The Maker Movement has come to third grade. These students have made what they call Droney, a wireless, radio-controlled, speech-synthesized flying robot that shoots marshmallows. I'm going to interview a few kids to find out

---

*It's okay to say "but," but we're not supposed to say "butt." Nobody knows why.

what they think."

"OOOOOOH!" shouted Andrea. "Pick me!"

Andrea waved her arms around like she was stranded on an island trying to signal a plane.

Of course, Ms. Beard picked Andrea.

"Tell us about the Maker Movement," Ms. Beard said, sticking the mic in Andrea's face.

"We printed our robot on a 3D printer," Andrea said, smiling into the camera. "Making things is so much fun! And it's educational too!"

What a brownnoser.

"How about you, little girl?" Ms. Beard

said, sticking the mic in Emily's face.

"I agree with everything Andrea said," said Emily.

Of *course*.

"I understand your drone is very intelligent," said Ms. Beard.

"Oh yes," said Mr. Klutz. "Droney even knows who invented the Band-Aid."

"IT WAS EARL DICKSON FROM NEW JERSEY," said Droney.

"Very impressive!" said Ms. Beard. "Can you sing a song, Droney?"

"CERTAINLY," replied Droney. "I CAN SING BETTER THAN ANY HUMAN BEING. AND I HAVE MEMORIZED EVERY SONG THAT EVER EXISTED."

"Droney is kind of conceited," I whispered to Ryan.

"*My* favorite song is from *Annie*," said Andrea, as if anybody asked.

"THE SUN WILL COME OUT, TOMORROW . . ." droned Droney.

Ugh. I hate that song.

"Very good!" said Mrs. Lilly as Droney kept singing the horrible song. "This is a *great* human-interest story. I'm going to put it in the newspaper."

"And I'm going to put it on TV," said Ms. Beard.

"YAY!" we all shouted, which is also "YAY" backward. Being on TV and in the newspaper will be cool.

That's when the weirdest thing in the history of the world happened.

But I'm not going to tell you what it was.

Okay, okay, I'll tell you. But you have to read the next chapter. So nah-nah-nah boo-boo on you!

We Created a Monster!

When Droney finished singing that horrible song, Miss Aker suggested we take it
outside for a test drive.

"THAT IS AN EXCELLENT IDEA!" said
Droney.

We all went out to the playground. Miss
Aker carried Droney and put it down

carefully in the middle of the blacktop. Ms. Beard's camera crew set up their equipment to shoot a video.

"This is gonna be cool," I said.

"Okay, Droney," said Miss Aker. "Show us what you can do. Go up!"

Droney's propellers started to spin and it made a humming noise. Slowly, the robot lifted up off the blacktop and hovered in the air about ten feet over our heads.

"Ooooh," everybody oooohed.

"Go left, Droney!" ordered Miss Aker. Droney moved left.

"Go right, Droney!" ordered Miss Aker. Droney moved right.

"Go up, Droney!" ordered Miss Aker.

Droney moved up.

"Go down, Droney!" ordered Miss Aker. Droney moved down.

It was *cool*. Ms. Beard's team got it all on video. Mrs. Lilly took notes and shot still pictures with her camera.

"As you can see, Droney is very maneuverable," said Miss Aker.

I didn't know what that meant, but Droney was darting back and forth all over the place even after Miss Aker stopped giving it voice commands. It was almost like Droney was showing off a little.

"Wow, look at it go!" shouted Ryan.

"That is *amazing*!" yelled Alexia.

Droney swooped down over our heads.

We ducked to get out of the way.

"The drone is getting a little too close to the students," said Mr. Klutz. "I'm afraid somebody might get hurt."

"Droney," hollered Miss Aker, "be careful not to—"

But she didn't have the chance to finish her sentence, because that's when the weirdest thing in the history of the world happened. Droney swooped down behind Mr. Klutz, hovered there for a second, and then grabbed the back of his shirt with its claw hand.

Then Droney lifted Mr. Klutz off the ground!

"What the—" shouted Mr. Klutz. "Ha ha,

very funny. Put me down, Droney!"

"Are you getting all this?" Ms. Beard shouted at her cameraman. "We are going live nationwide!"

"Droney, what are you doing?" shouted Miss Aker.

"I AM NOW IN CHARGE," announced Droney as it dangled Mr. Klutz over our heads.

"Ha ha," laughed Miss Aker. "Uh . . . what do you mean?"

"I AM THE NEW PRINCIPAL FOR LIFE," replied Droney. "THEN I WILL BE PRESI-DENT OF THE BOARD OF EDUCATION. THEN I WILL BECOME KING OF THE WORLD! BWA-HA-HA!"

Oh no! Droney said "Bwa-ha-ha." You know what *that* means. The only ones who ever say "Bwa-ha-ha" are evil psycho- paths. That's the first rule of being an evil psychopath.

"NOOOOOOOOO!" we all shouted.

"Let him go!" shouted Ryan.

"Help!" hollered Mr. Klutz. "Help!"

Ms. Beard and Mrs. Lilly rubbed their hands together with excitement.

"This is great!" said Ms. Beard. "I bet I can make this into a miniseries!"

"I can see the headline now," said Mrs. Lilly. "PRINCIPAL KIDNAPPED BY INSANE DRONE!"

Ms. Beard ran in front of the camera.

"This is Ms. Beard, reporting live from Ella Mentry School," she said. "I have breaking news. Droney, a wireless, radio-controlled, speech-synthesized flying robot drone has taken the principal captive. I'm going to try to interview the principal now. How do you feel, Mr. Klutz?"

"Terrible!" shouted Mr. Klutz. "Help me!"

"Can you put a little more emotion into it?" asked Ms. Beard.

"Get your claw hand off me!" Mr. Klutz shouted at Droney.

"Much better!" yelled Ms. Beard.

But Droney didn't let go of Mr. Klutz. It flew higher.

"BWA-HA-HA!" said Droney.

"Droney is *evil*!" shouted Alexia. "We created a monster!"

"Help!" shouted Mr. Klutz. "Oww, my arm!"

"We've got to *do* something!" shouted Emily.

"Let's throw rocks at it!" shouted Neil. "Maybe we can hit one of the propellers and knock Droney out of the sky!"

The guys and I rushed to pick up rocks near the playground. I'm good at throwing stuff.

"No! Wait!" shouted Andrea. "You might hit Mr. Klutz!"

"DO NOT TRY TO STOP ME, OR MR. KLUTZ WILL GET HURT!" said Droney.

Andrea wheeled around and turned to me.

"This is all *your* fault, Arlo!" she yelled.

"My fault?" I said. "What did *I* do?"

"It was *your* idea to make a robot on the 3D printer," yelled Andrea.

"It was not!"

"Was too!"

We went back and forth like that for a while.

"Ooooh, A.J. and Andrea are bickering," said Ryan. "They must be in *love*!"

"When are you gonna get married?" asked Michael.

Droney kept rising higher in the air, with Mr. Klutz dangling below it.

"Are you getting all this on video?" Ms. Beard asked her crew. "It's going to be *great* for the ratings!"

"I can see the headline now," said Mrs. Lilly. "MAKER MOVEMENT AMOK!"

And at that moment, Droney flew away.

"Help!" shouted Mr. Klutz. "HELLLLL-LLLLPPPPPPP!"

We all watched as Droney and Mr. Klutz disappeared into the distance.

Nobody said anything for a long time. You could have heard a pin drop on the playground.*

Droney was gone, and it took Mr. Klutz with him. We were all sad. Some kids were crying.

Ms. Beard turned to face the camera.

"We'll be right back," she said, "after this important message . . ."

---

*That was weird. Why would anybody bring pins to school?

An Important Message . . .

7

Parents! Teachers! Librarians! Are you tired of seeing so much graphic violins in children's books? This can be very harmful, and it sets a bad example for kids.

On the next two pages is a scene of graphic violins. If you don't like graphic violins, hide your eyes! Young children should not be allowed to see these horrible images.*

---

*Don't turn the page! Don't do it! Oh no, you're turning the page!

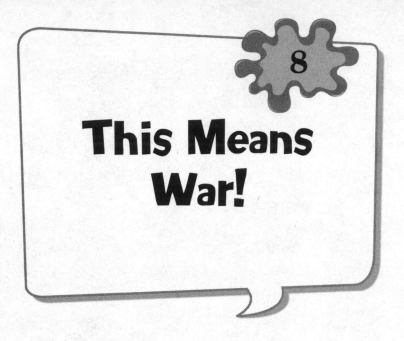

This Means War!

After Droney kidnapped Mr. Klutz, we all ran inside. We closed the door of the Fab Lab behind us.

"Quick, lock the door!" said Miss Aker. "Droney could come back any minute!"

I was all out of breath and panting, which means I was wearing pants.

"We've got to *do* something!" shouted Emily.

"What are we gonna do?" asked Ryan.

"We have to rescue Mr. Klutz," said Neil.

"To do that," said Miss Aker, "we're going to have to take drastic measures."

"Like what?" we all asked.

"The only thing we *can* do," said Miss Aker. "We're going to have to . . . destroy Droney."

"GASP!" we all gasped.

We had worked so hard to make Droney, it would be a shame to destroy it. But Miss Aker was right. There was no choice.

Suddenly, we heard a knock at the door of the Fab Lab.

"Don't open that door!" I shouted.

"Why not?" asked Andrea.

"In scary movies," I explained, "whenever there's a knock on a door and they open it, some maniac comes in. Droney might be hovering right outside the door!"

"That's ridiculous, Arlo," said Andrea. "There's no maniac on the other side of the door. Right, Miss Aker?"

Miss Aker went over and opened the door slowly. And you'll never believe in a million hundred years who was standing there.

I'm not going to tell you.

Okay, okay, I'll tell you. It was Officer Spence, our school security guard!

"Officer Spence!" we all shouted.

"We're so glad you're here," said Miss Aker.

"Duty calls!" said Officer Spence.

Me and the guys started giggling because Officer Spence said "duty," which sounds just like "doody" even though they're spelled differently.*

"Officer Spence will know what to do," said Andrea. "He's a trained policeman."

"What's the problem?" asked Officer Spence.

"We made a robot drone that shoots marshmallows," explained Miss Aker. "It kidnapped Mr. Klutz and took him away. The drone says it is principal for life, and it wants to take over the world."

"Hmmmm," said Officer Spence, as if this sort of thing happened all the time. "That's the problem with robot drones. They always want to take over the world."

---

*It's fine to say "duty," but we're not supposed to say "doody." Nobody knows why.

I guess that's the first rule of robot drones.

"What should we do?" asked Alexia.

"Well," said Officer Spence, "the only way to stop a bad guy shooting marshmallows is with a good guy shooting marshmallows."

"We're makers, right?" said Miss Aker. "We can make marshmallow shooters! It's easy! We need to make as many as we can, and as quickly as we can before Droney comes back."

"Yeah!" we all shouted.

Miss Aker had a big box filled with PVC pipe, those plastic tubes that plumbers use on sinks. She showed us how to cut the PVC pipe and tape the pieces together to make a cool-looking marshmallow shooter.

Everybody pitched in, and we rushed to make a marshmallow shooter for each of us.

"This means war!" I said as I put my PVC pipe together.

"I don't approve of violence," Andrea

said, "but desperate times call for desperate measures."

"What do you have against violins?" I asked.

"Not violins, Arlo!" Andrea yelled at me. "Violence!"

I was just yanking Andrea's chain. I noticed that Miss Aker had a worried look on her face.

"What's wrong, Miss Aker?" I asked.

"I don't think these marshmallow shooters are going to be enough to stop Droney," she replied. "We're going to need more firepower."

"We could make a soda-bottle airplane," said Ryan.

"We could make a solar blimp, or a rubber-band helicopter," said Michael.

"We could make friendship necklaces," said Emily.

"What good would *that* do?" I asked.

"I have an idea," said Alexia. "Why don't we make another drone?"

Another drone! Yes!

"We could make a drone that's bigger and stronger and meaner than Droney," said Alexia.

It was a genius idea! Alexia should get the Nobel Prize for that one.

We got to work right away making another drone. Miss Aker called Mr. Docker and Mrs. Yonkers down to the Fab Lab to help with the computer stuff.

Some of the other teachers came down too. Everybody pitched in. We knew we would have to work as a team to defeat Droney.

I noticed that our own teacher, Mr. Cooper, wasn't there.

"Hey, where's Mr. Cooper?"

"I asked him to come," said Mrs. Yonkers. "He said he didn't want to."

"I think Mr. Cooper is in a bad mood," said Andrea, "because we're always working in the Fab Lab and we never finish our math lesson."

We all worked really hard on the new drone. Mr. Docker drew the basic design. Mrs. Yonkers programmed the computer stuff.

"Can we make the new drone more modest than Droney?" asked Andrea.

"Yeah, Droney was kind of conceited," said Neil.

"Good idea," said Miss Aker. Mrs. Yonkers agreed. Instead of downloading the *entire* internet into the new drone, she only put in the *good* parts.

The new drone was nearly finished. We were printing it on the 3D printer when there was a knock on the door. I told Miss Aker not to open it, but she did anyway. And you'll never believe who was standing there.

I'm not going to tell you.

Okay, okay, I'll tell you. It was a bunch of PTA moms! And they were holding plates filled with homemade brownies and peanut butter and jelly sandwiches.

"Thank you!" said Miss Aker.

She gathered us all around her as we ate brownies and peanut butter and jelly sandwiches.

"This was your finest hour," she said. "Never in the field of human conflict was so much owed by so many to so few."

I had no idea what she was talking about. But finally, our new robot drone was finished. It just needed one more thing—a name. We shouted out lots of names—New Improved Droney. Droney 2.0. Droney Destroyer.

"How about . . . Super Droney?" suggested Alexia.

"Yeah!" everybody shouted. We all agreed that Super Droney would be a cool name.

"Speak, Super Droney," said Miss Aker.

Super Droney said just three words.

"MUST . . . DESTROY . . . DRONEY."

D-Day

Miss Aker picked up Super Droney. We grabbed our marshmallow shooters and gathered up as many bags of marshmallows as we could carry.

"It's D-Day, kids," Miss Aker said very seriously. "That stands for Droney Day. Let's *do* this."

We marched out to the playground.

When we got there, I looked up in the sky. There was no sign of Droney or Mr. Klutz. The teachers started digging foxholes in the dirt around the playground. Miss Aker hid Super Droney behind the slide.

"Super Droney will be our secret weapon," she said.

"MUST . . . DESTROY . . . DRONEY," repeated Super Droney.

Miss Aker led us over to a picnic table and unrolled a big map on it. We all gathered around. So did Ms. Beard and Mrs. Lilly.

"Droney will probably come from *this* direction," Miss Aker said, pointing at the map. "We'll wait until it gets *here*, and if Droney comes down low enough, we'll attack it with marshmallows *here."*

Miss Aker looked like she was in complete control. I was nervous. We all were. I loaded a marshmallow into my shooter.

"I'm scared," said Emily, who is always scared.

"Remember kids," Miss Aker told us. "We are makers. We will defend our school, whatever the cost may be. We will fight on the beaches. We will fight on the landing grounds. We will fight in the fields and in the streets. We will fight in the hills. We will *never* surrender!"

Miss Aker was very inspirational.

"Are you kids with me?" she asked.

"Yeah!" we all shouted.

Miss Aker took out binoculars and

scanned the horizon. There was no sign of Droney.

"What if Droney doesn't come back?" asked Michael.

"Oh, it will come back," Miss Aker reassured him. "It wants to be principal of the school. It *has* to come back. And when it does, we're going to blast it out of the sky. I just hope we brought along enough marshmallows."

There was nothing to do but wait. We all climbed into foxholes. In the distance, I heard somebody playing a harmonica. That's when Andrea came over. She got into my foxhole with me.

"What are you doing here?" I whispered. "Get your own foxhole."

"Arlo," she whispered, "I need to talk to you."

"About what?" I whispered.

"Just in case one of us doesn't make it out of here alive," Andrea whispered, "I want you to know something."

"What?" I whispered.

"Arlo, I just want you to know—"

But Andrea didn't have the chance to finish her sentence, because Miss Aker started yelling.

"Look, up in the sky!" she shouted. "It's Droney!"

I looked up. There was a dot in the distant sky. Andrea jumped out of my foxhole and climbed into another one.

"Droney is coming this way!" shouted Ryan.

"Does it have Mr. Klutz with it?" asked Emily.

"I don't think so," said Ryan. "It's too far away to tell."

"Okay, get ready, everyone," said Miss Aker. "When Droney gets close enough, we're going to give it everything we've got. But don't shoot until you see the whites of the propellers."

Droney came closer . . . and closer . . .

until it hovered over the playground, just a little too high for us to reach with our marshmallow shooters.

"SO, WE MEET AGAIN," said Droney.

"Where is Mr. Klutz?" shouted Miss Aker.

"THAT IS FOR ME TO KNOW AND YOU TO FIND OUT," replied Droney. "PUT DOWN YOUR PATHETIC MARSHMAL-LOW SHOOTERS."

How dare Droney insult our marshmal-low shooters! We made them with our own hands.

Well, it would be hard to make some-thing with somebody *else's* hands.

"We'll put down our marshmallow shooters when you return Mr. Klutz," shouted Miss Aker.

"NO DEAL," replied Droney.

"Then you leave us no choice," said Miss Aker. "Super Droney, go *get* him!"

There was a humming sound as Super Droney's propellers started to spin. It rose up from behind the slide.

"MUST . . . DESTROY . . . DRONEY," said Super Droney.

"SO," said Droney, "I SEE YOU MADE ANOTHER DRONE. VERY CLEVER. BUT IT WON'T WORK!"

Droney faced Super Droney as both drones hovered over our heads.

"YOU'RE A MAKER?" Droney said. "GO AHEAD. MAKE MY DAY!"

"WITH PLEASURE!" replied Super Droney.

I'm not sure which one of them shot first. But the next thing we knew, the air was filled with marshmallows as Droney and Super Droney shot at each other with their rapid-fire marshmallow shooters.

It was a dogfight in the sky. You should have been there! Mrs. Lilly and Ms. Beard were recording everything, but we got to see it with our own eyes.

Well, it would be pretty hard to see it with somebody else's eyes.

Marshmallows were raining down from the sky. I stuffed a few in my pockets and a few in my mouth, because my parents always tell me not to waste food. Also, I love marshmallows.

Droney and Super Droney were both really fast, zipping back and forth as they fired marshmallows at each other. Neither of them made a direct hit. I knew that if one of them managed to hit the other's propeller, it would be all over. There was electricity in the air.

Well, not really. If there had been electricity in the air, we would have been electrocuted.

But we were on the edge of our seats!

Well, not really. There are no seats in the playground.

But it was really exciting!

"You can do it, Super Droney!" I shouted.

"Dodge! Duck! Dip! Dive!" shouted Miss Aker.

We had built Super Droney to be bigger and faster than Droney, and it looked like it was winning.

"GIVE UP, DRONEY!" said Super Droney.

"WHO'S GONNA MAKE ME?" replied Droney.

"*We* made you!" shouted Miss Aker. "We're *makers*."

The battle raged on. Super Droney was getting off some good shots, and there was a near miss as one of the marshmallows passed within inches of Droney's propeller. And then, suddenly, Droney, moving sideways, fired a shot. The marshmallow

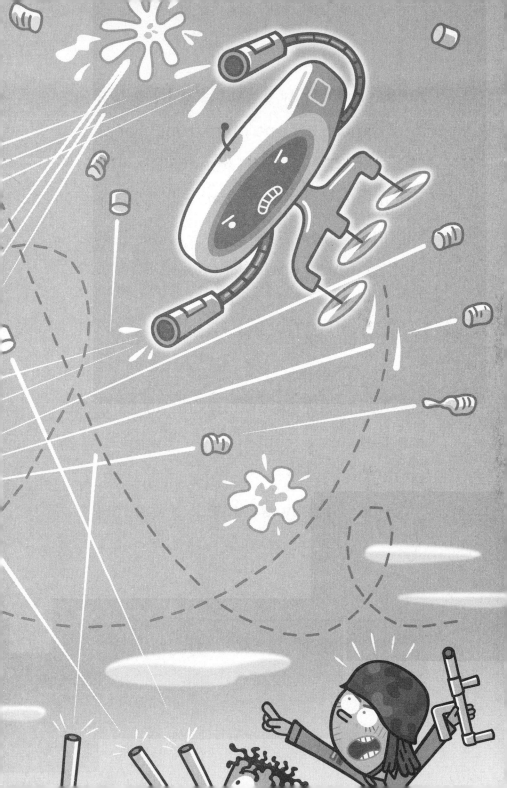

hit Super Droney in the face, bounced off, and glanced off one of its front propellers.

"I AM HIT!" Super Droney said.

"Oh *noooooooooooooooooo*!" somebody shouted.

"It's coming down!" hollered Miss Aker. "Watch out!"

"Run for your lives!" shouted Neil.

Super Droney fell from the sky and crashed to the ground upside down about ten feet away from me. It couldn't fly. It couldn't speak.*

"Super Droney is totaled!" I shouted.

---

*Pretty exciting, huh? But wait until you read the next chapter!

The Big Surprise Ending

I peeked out of my foxhole. Super Droney was on the ground, in pieces. Our secret weapon had been destroyed.

"BWA-HA-HA!" said Droney as it hovered over our heads. "YOU THOUGHT YOU COULD DEFEAT ME BY MAKING SOME FLIMSY MARSHMALLOW SHOOTERS AND A PATHETIC DRONE?"

I looked at Miss Aker. Andrea looked at Miss Aker. Ryan looked at Miss Aker. Emily looked at Miss Aker.

In case you were wondering, everybody was looking at Miss Aker.

"What do we do *now*?" asked Andrea.

"We attack!" Miss Aker yelled as she climbed out of her foxhole. "Follow me, kids! We have nothing to fear but fear itself! *Charge!*"

CHARGE!

We all climbed out of our foxholes and followed Miss Aker toward Droney.

"Fire!" shouted Miss Aker. "Hit it with everything you've got!"

I fired a marshmallow, and then reloaded my marshmallow shooter. The air was filled with marshmallows. Droney dodged them and fired marshmallows back.

"Victory at all costs!" Miss Aker shouted as she led us into battle. "Never give in. Never give up!"

"We're running out of marshmallows!" shouted Ryan.

"Somebody needs to go to the super-market and buy more!" shouted Michael.

"No time for that!" Miss Aker shouted as she turned around. "It's now or never!"

And then, just as she turned back around, a marshmallow hit Miss Aker in the face.

"I'm hit!" she shouted as she stumbled to the ground.

We all gathered around Miss Aker.

"He . . . got me," she groaned, covering her eye with one hand.

That was weird. I mean, it was just a marshmallow.

"You'll be okay," said Andrea, trying to help Miss Aker up.

"No," she moaned. "You kids are going to have to carry on without me, I'm afraid. The Maker Movement must continue, even if I can't."

Miss Aker fell back on the ground. Emily

started crying. I thought I might cry too.

"What are we gonna do *now*?" asked Neil.

"BWA-HA-HA!" said Droney. "YOU MADE ME. BUT YOUR SILLY MAKER MOVEMENT IS *OVER.*"

Droney was right. All hope was lost. Super Droney was destroyed. Mr. Klutz was missing. Miss Aker was injured. We were going to have to surrender to Droney.

That's when the weirdest thing in the history of the world happened. You'll

never believe who came running out to the playground at that moment.

I'm not going to tell you.

Okay, okay. I'll tell you.

It was Mr. Cooper!

"WHO . . . IS . . . THAT?" asked Droney.

"He's our teacher!" we shouted.

Mr. Cooper was carrying the violin he had been playing at his desk.*

"Step aside, everyone!" shouted Mr. Cooper. "*I'll* handle this!"

"What are you going to do?" asked Ryan.

"I'm part of the Maker Movement too," Mr. Cooper yelled. "And I converted my violin into a weapon!"**

---

*There sure are a lot of violins in this book.
**Don't try this at home, kids! You'll break your instrument.

He took the bow of his violin and attached the end of it to the strings. Then he pulled back the strings. He pointed the bow at the sky like he was shooting an arrow. And then, suddenly . . .

Twaaaaannnnnggggg!

The bow shot up into the sky.

It slammed into Droney, right in the propeller! Direct hit!

"OHHHHHHH!" said Droney as it started to wobble crazily. "YOU CURSED BRATS! LOOK WHAT YOU'VE DONE! OH, WHAT A WORLD! WHO WOULD HAVE THOUGHT KIDS

LIKE YOU COULD DESTROY MY BEAUTI-
FUL WICKEDNESS!"

Droney was falling!

"OHHH! LOOK OUT! OHH-
HHHH!"

Droney slammed into
the monkey bars and shat-
tered into a million hundred
pieces.

"GASP!" we all gasped.

For a moment or two, there
was silence. And then . . .

"Hooray for Mr. Cooper!"
everybody shouted.

"He saved the world!" I
shouted.

* * *

Well, that's pretty much what happened. I guess Mr. Cooper *is* a real superhero after all.

A few minutes later, Mr. Klutz came stumbling back to school, his shirt and pants all ripped. We gave him a big hug. Everybody was happy as we went back into school and filed into our classroom. Well, everybody was happy except for Andrea, *of course*.

"I don't approve of all this violence," said Andrea.

"What do you have against violins?" I asked.

"Not violins, Arlo!" shouted Andrea. "Violence!"

"Okay, everyone, " said Mr. Cooper. "We

have a lot of work to make up. Turn to page twenty-three in your math books."

Noooooooooooooo!

The next day, the story of how we built Droney and destroyed it was all over the TV news and in the newspaper. It was turned into a six-part miniseries on Netflix. We were on the cover of *Make* magazine.

Maybe Miss Aker will recover from getting hit in the eye with a marshmallow. Maybe dogs will stop taking elevators. Maybe Andrea will finish what she wanted to tell me in the foxhole. Maybe I'll lick a bowling alley. Maybe people will stop talking about cake and walking into doors all the time. Maybe Mr. Klutz will get some dolphins for the all-porpoise room.

But it won't be easy!

Do you like making stuff? The Maker Movement is a real thing! You'll get lots of ideas if you go online and search for "maker projects for kids."

More weird books from Dan Gutman

My Weird School

My Weird School Graphic Novels

My Weirder School

My Weirdest School

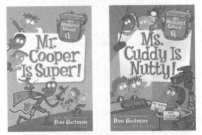

My Weirder-est School

My Weird School Fast Facts

My Weird School Daze

My Weird Tips

HARPER
An Imprint of HarperCollinsPublishers

harpercollinschildrens.com